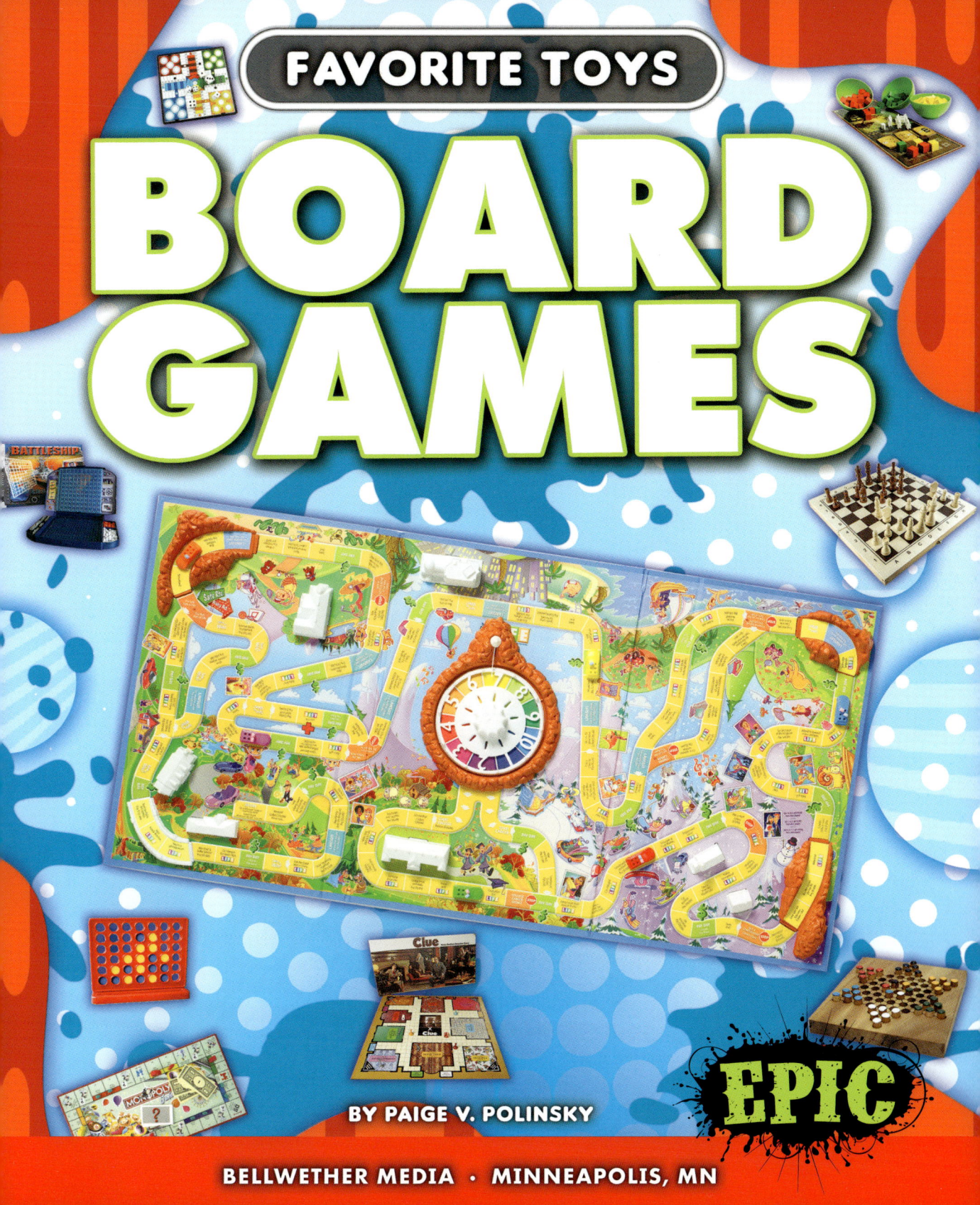

FAVORITE TOYS
BOARD GAMES

BY PAIGE V. POLINSKY

EPIC

BELLWETHER MEDIA • MINNEAPOLIS, MN

EPIC

Action and adventure collide in EPIC. Plunge into a universe of powerful beasts, hair-raising tales, and high-speed excitement. Astonishing explorations await. Can you handle it?

This edition first published in 2023 by Bellwether Media, Inc.

No part of this publication may be reproduced in whole or in part without written permission of the publisher. For information regarding permission, write to Bellwether Media, Inc., Attention: Permissions Department, 6012 Blue Circle Drive, Minnetonka, MN 55343.

Library of Congress Cataloging-in-Publication Data

LC record for Board Games available at: https://lccn.loc.gov/2022004842

Text copyright © 2023 by Bellwether Media, Inc. EPIC and associated logos are trademarks and/or registered trademarks of Bellwether Media, Inc.

Editor: Elizabeth Neuenfeldt   Designer: Josh Brink

Printed in the United States of America, North Mankato, MN.

TABLE OF CONTENTS

Game On!..................................4
The History of........................6
   Board Games
Board Games Today...............16
More Than a Toy..................20
Glossary................................22
To Learn More......................23
Index....................................24

Game On!

A family sits around a table. They pass out money and roll dice. Their **tokens** race around a colorful board.

It does not matter who wins. Everyone loves board game night!

The History of Board Games

Strategy games have been popular for centuries. *Senet* is one of the earliest. This Egyptian game dates back to around 3100 BCE!

Early board game pieces were often made of bones, sticks, and stones.

SENET

BOARD GAME BEGINNINGS

Egypt = 🔴

THE KING OF GAMES

EARLY CHESS WAS CALLED *CHATURANGA*. IT APPEARED IN INDIA BETWEEN 500 AND 600 CE. CHESS IS NOW THE BEST-SELLING BOARD GAME OF ALL TIME!

In the 1500s, the *Game of the Goose* was popular in Italy. Players rolled dice to move around the board.

GAME OF THE GOOSE

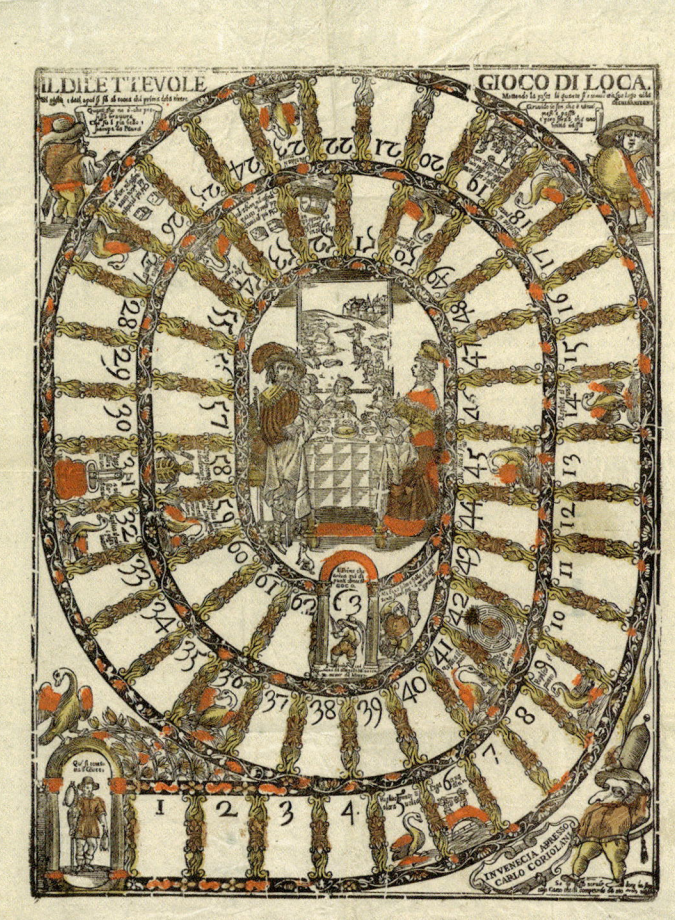

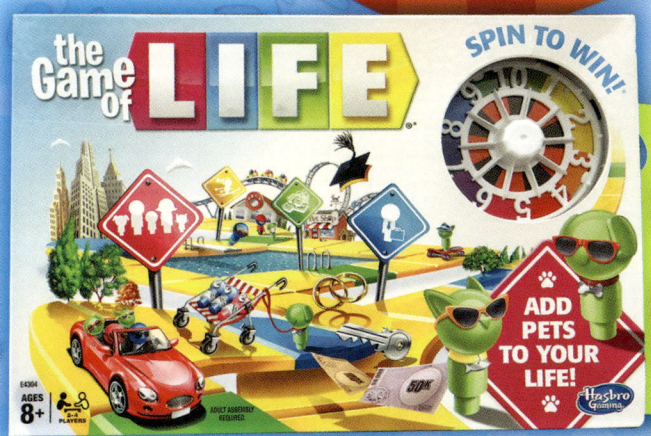

REUBEN'S LIFE

REUBEN KLAMER REMADE *THE CHECKERED GAME OF LIFE* IN 1960. TODAY, *THE GAME OF LIFE* HAS A FRESH NEW LOOK. IT USES A SPINNING WHEEL!

THE CHECKERED GAME OF LIFE

In 1860, Milton Bradley made *The Checkered Game of Life*. This **game of chance** was popular!

In 1904, Elizabeth Magie **patented** *The Landlord's Game*. Players bought and sold **real estate**.

THE LANDLORD'S GAME

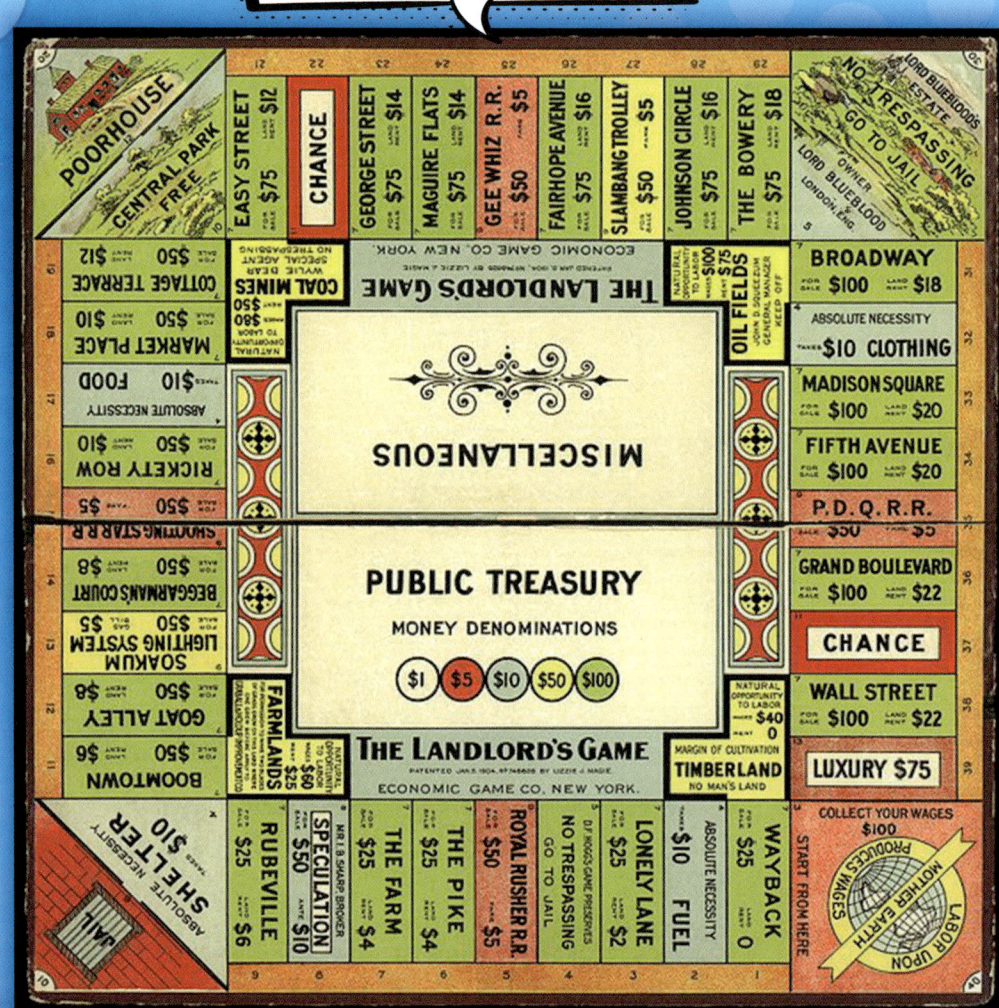

Charles Darrow sold his own version of it to Parker Brothers in 1935. It was called *Monopoly*. The game was a hit!

Alfred Butts and James Brunot first sold *Scrabble* in 1948. This word game became a family favorite!

In 1949, *Clue* was first sold. Many loved this mysterious strategy game!

ALFRED BUTTS

ONE SWEET TEACHER

A teacher named Eleanor Abbot created *Candy Land* in 1948. She made it for kids in the San Diego hospital.

In 1957, Albert Lamorisse created *The Conquest of the World*. This French strategy game became *Risk*.

In 1995, Klaus Teuber released *Settlers of Catan* in Germany. Players competed to build roads and cities.

KLAUS TEUBER

SETTLERS OF CATAN

TOP SELLER SETTLERS!

TODAY, MORE THAN 32 MILLION COPIES OF *SETTLERS OF CATAN* HAVE BEEN SOLD!

BOARD GAME TIMELINE

1860 Milton Bradley creates *The Checkered Game of Life*

1904 Elizabeth Magie creates *The Landlord's Game*

1948 *Scrabble* is first sold

1949 *Clue* is first sold

1995 *Settlers of Catan* is released

RISK

15

Board Games Today

Players still play older games. New versions are often based on movies or video games. People also like newer games. In **cooperative games**, players work together to win. **Legacy games** let players change the game board!

BOARD GAMES TYPES

**The Game of Life
(game of chance)**

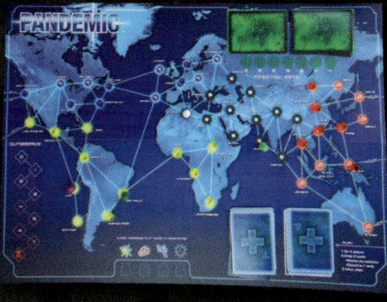

**Pandemic
(cooperative game)**

**Monopoly
(strategy game)**

**Scrabble
(word game)**

17

Today's board games are extra exciting. Some have **apps** so people can play almost anywhere.

GAME APPS

BOARD GAME PUBLISHER

Board game fans also **publish** their own games. New games are created every day!

More Than a Toy

Players **stream** themselves playing board games online. Others create YouTube videos to teach games to new players.

Fans meet at **conventions** and fairs. They can try the newest games. Board games bring people together!

ESSEN GAME FAIR PROFILE

What Is It? A board game fair that presents board games from around the world

Where Is It? Essen, Germany

When Did It Start? 1983

When Does It Happen? Once a year every October

ESSEN GAME FAIR

Glossary

apps—programs or games that can be downloaded onto mobile devices

conventions—events where fans of a subject meet

cooperative games—games where players work together to win

game of chance—a game in which luck rather than skill causes the outcome of the game

legacy games—games where the board is changed permanently as it is played, usually by placing stickers on game pieces

patented—gained the legal right to be the only person to make or sell an invention

publish—to release to the public

real estate—relating to the business of selling land and buildings

strategy games—games that require careful planning to achieve goals

stream—to make videos live online

tokens—game pieces

To Learn More

AT THE LIBRARY

Kemmeter, Jennifer. *Chess for Kids: An Interactive Guide to the World's Greatest Game.* New York City, N.Y.: Black Dog & Leventhal, 2022.

Polinsky, Paige. *Toy Cars.* Minneapolis, Minn.: Bellwether Media, 2023.

Stone, Tanya Lee. *Pass Go and Collect $200: The Real Story of How Monopoly Was Invented.* New York City, N.Y.: Henry Holt & Company, 2018.

ON THE WEB

Factsurfer.com gives you a safe, fun way to find more information.

1. Go to www.factsurfer.com.

2. Enter "board games" into the search box and click 🔍.

3. Select your book cover to see a list of related content.

Index

Abbot, Eleanor, 13
apps, 18
beginnings, 7
Bradley, Milton, 9
Brunot, James, 12
Butts, Alfred, 12
Candy Land, 13
Checkered Game of Life, The, 9
chess, 7
Clue, 12, 13
Conquest of the World, The, 14
conventions, 20
Darrow, Charles, 11
Essen Game Fair, 21
fairs, 20
Game of Life, The, 9
Game of the Goose, 8

history, 6, 7, 8, 9, 10, 11, 12, 13, 14
Klamer, Reuben, 9
Lamorisse, Albert, 14
Landlord's Game, The, 10
Magie, Elizabeth, 10
Monopoly, 5, 11
Parker Brothers, 11
publish, 19
Risk, 14, 15
sales, 7, 14
Scrabble, 12
Senet, 6
Settlers of Catan, 14
stream, 20
Teuber, Klaus, 14
timeline, 15
types, 6, 9, 12, 14, 16, 17
YouTube videos, 20

The images in this book are reproduced through the courtesy of: Judith Collins/ Alamy, cover (hero); urbanbuzz, cover (Monopoly), pp. 3 (Monopoly car), 4 (Monopoly money); Page Light Studios, cover (Clue), pp. 13 (Clue), 22; Maxim Tupikov, cover (Chinese Checkers); Will Thomass, cover (Chess); Izabela Krecioch, cover (Century: A New World); Pao Laroid, cover (figures); KerrysWorld, cover (Battleship); Anastasia Sokolenko, back cover (Monopoly hat and dog), pp. 5 (Monopoly tokens), 11 (Monopoly tokens); Branislav Carven, back cover (Sorry!); Jiri Hera, back cover (red pawn); Viktoriia Kotliarchuk, p. 2 (Backgammon); Red Herring, p. 3 (Yahtzee); CaseyMartin, p. 4 (Monopoly cards); Mr.Note19, p. 5 (family); World History Archive/ Alamy, p. 6; Seregam, p. 7 (Chess); Universal Images Group Editorial/ Getty Images, p. 8; ZikG, pp. 9 (The Game of Life), 16 (Toy Story); http://chnm.gmu.edu/ Wiki Commons, p. 9; Thomas Forsyth/Landlords-Game.Info/ Wiki Commons, p. 10; PA/ Alamy, p. 11 (Charles Darrow); Hulton Archive/ Getty Images, p. 12; Chris Wilson/ Alamy, p. 13 (Candy Land); dpa picture alliance/ Alamy, p. 14; Science History Images, p. 15 (Milton Bradley); Ben Molyneux/ Alamy, p. 15 (Risk); Lokibaho, p. 15 (Settlers of Catan); vvoe, p. 17 (The Game of Life); LightField Studios, p. 17 (Monopoly); eugenehill, p. 17 (Scrabble); Jr images, p. 18 (hand / left phone); Elizabeth Neuenfeldt/ Bellwether Media, p. 18 (left phone screen); Daniel VG, p. 18 (right phone); ZUMA Press/ Alamy, p. 19; Sean Dempsey, p. 20; Ulrich Baumgarten/ Getty Images, pp. 20-21.